AMAZING MILITARY MACHINES

MILITARY SHIPS AND SUBMARINES

by Mari Schuh

PEBBLE
a capstone imprint

Dedicated to Dan Ruemping

Published by Pebble, an imprint of Capstone.
1710 Roe Crest Drive, North Mankato, Minnesota 56003
capstonepub.com

Copyright © 2023 by Capstone. All rights reserved. No part of this publication may be reproduced in whole or in part, or stored in a retrieval system, or transmitted in any form or by any means, electronic, mechanical, photocopying, recording, or otherwise, without written permission of the publisher.

Library of Congress Cataloging-in-Publication Data
Names: Schuh, Mari C., 1975- author.
Title: Military ships and submarines / Mari Schuh.
Description: North Mankato, Minnesota : Pebble, an imprint of Capstone, [2023] | Series: Amazing military machines | Includes bibliographical references. | Audience: Ages 5-8 | Audience: Grades K-1 | Summary: "Militaries use amazing vehicles on the water. Aircraft carriers and submarines are just a few of the mighty military machines that get the job done!"— Provided by publisher.
Identifiers: LCCN 2021059273 (print) | LCCN 2021059274 (ebook) | ISBN 9781666350302 (hardcover) | ISBN 9781666350340 (paperback) | ISBN 9781666350388 (pdf) | ISBN 9781666350463 (kindle edition)
Subjects: LCSH: Warships—Juvenile literature. | Submarines (Ships)—Juvenile literature. | Aircraft carriers—Juvenile literature. | CYAC: Warships. | Submarines (Ships) | Aircraft carriers.
Classification: LCC V765 .S43 2023 (print) | LCC V765 (ebook) | DDC 359.8/3—dc23/eng/20211220
LC record available at https://lccn.loc.gov/2021059273
LC ebook record available at https://lccn.loc.gov/2021059274

Image Credits
Shutterstock: Adriana_R, 17, Kuleshov Oleg, 8, Lertsakwiman, 20, offstocker, 20; U.S. Navy photo by Mass Communication Specialist 1st Class William Spears, 6, MC2 Andrew J. Sneeringer, 7, MC2 Christian Senyk/Released, 5, MC3 Kaysee Lohmann, Cover, MC3 Class Michael C. Barton/Released, 11, Petty Officer 3rd Class John Wagner, 14, PO3 Jonathan Sunderman, 15, PO3 Kyle Goldberg/Released, 19; Wikimedia: Bellona Foundation, 9, Crown Copyright/LA(Phot) Jay Allen, 13, U.S. Navy photo, 18

Editorial Credits
Editor: Erika L. Shores; Designer: Dina Her; Media Researcher: Jo Miller; Production Specialist: Tori Abraham

All internet sites appearing in back matter were available and accurate when this book was sent to press.

TABLE OF CONTENTS

Super Ships 4

USS *Gerald R. Ford* 6

Typhoon 8

Mercy 10

Mine Hunters 12

Destroyers 14

Zubr 16

Big Decks 18

    Make a Toy Boat 20

    Glossary 22

    Read More 23

    Internet Sites 23

    Index 24

    About the Author 24

Words in **bold** are in the glossary.

SUPER SHIPS

Military ships and **submarines** are strong and fast. Aircraft carriers hold jets and helicopters. **Mine** hunters search the sea. These vehicles are on the move!

USS GERALD R. FORD

The USS *Gerald R. Ford* is a huge aircraft carrier. It weighs almost 100,000 tons. That is as much as 400 Statues of Liberty.

This aircraft carrier is like a floating city.
More than 4,000 people work on it.
The large deck holds 75 aircraft.
Aircraft land and take off from the deck.

TYPHOON

The Typhoon is the biggest submarine in the world. It is longer than a football field. It is three times as tall as a house.

Submarines travel underwater. Many travel for 30 days or longer. The Typhoon can travel in the ocean for 120 days. **Nuclear power** helps the Typhoon move quickly.

MERCY

Mercy is a hospital ship that travels to areas around the world. It has 1,000 hospital beds. The ship is used to help people after **natural disasters**.

More than 1,300 people can work on the ship. Ten elevators transport them to the ship's different areas.

MINE HUNTERS

Hunt Class ships are mine hunters. They look for mines on the ocean floor. Then they destroy the mines. This keeps the ocean safe for other ships.

The ships use **sonar** to sense faraway objects. They can find an object the size of a football that is 3,200 feet (975 meters) away!

DESTROYERS

Arleigh Burke destroyers are warships. They are about 500 feet (152 m) long. Each ship can hold more than 300 crew members.

These destroyers go on **missions** alone or as part of a group. Each destroyer can hold more than 90 missiles. **Radar** and sonar help the ship find targets.

ZUBR

The Zubr is the largest hovercraft in the world. It is 187 feet (57 m) long. It can carry 360 troops or three battle tanks. Moving on a cushion of air, it travels short distances. It delivers troops and vehicles to beaches.

BIG DECKS

Big decks look like small aircraft carriers. They carry helicopters and fighter jets. These ships are also called amphibious assault ships.

Big decks can help out quickly when they are needed. They often help after natural disasters. They are among the amazing vehicles sailing the seas around the world.

MAKE A TOY BOAT

What You Need

- chopstick
- egg carton
- glue
- ribbon or string
- scissors
- paint or markers
- paper

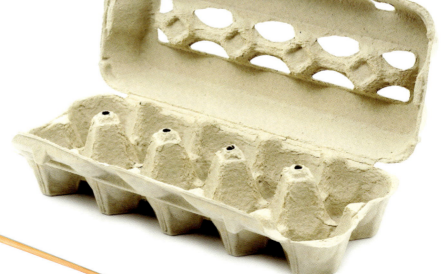

What You Do

1. Using the chopstick, make a hole in the middle of the egg carton. Add glue so the chopstick doesn't easily move. The chopstick will be your boat's mast.

2. Loop a piece of ribbon around the chopstick and then around the egg carton. Tie the ribbon under the egg carton. Add glue, if needed. The ribbon will help keep the chopstick pointing up.

3. Color or paint a sheet of paper. Fold it to make a triangle. Fold the paper around the chopstick. Glue the paper in place. The paper will be your boat's sail.

GLOSSARY

mine (MINE)—a type of bomb

mission (MISH-uhn)—a planned job or task

natural disaster (NACH-ur-uhl di-ZAS-tuhr)—an earthquake, flood, storm, or other deadly event caused by nature

nuclear power (NOO-klee-ur POW-ur)—power created by splitting atoms

radar (RAY-dar)—a device that uses radio waves to track the location of objects

sonar (SOH-nar)—a device that uses sound waves to find underwater objects

submarine (SUHB-muh-reen)—a ship that can travel underwater

READ MORE

London, Martha. *Military Ships*. Minneapolis: DiscoverRoo, an imprint of Pop!, 2020.

Ransom, Candice. *How Aircraft Carriers Work*. Minneapolis: Lerner Publications, 2020.

Rossiter, Brienna. *Big Machines in the Military*. Lake Elmo, MN: Focus Readers, 2021.

INTERNET SITES

Kiddle: Ship Facts for Kids
kids.kiddle.co/Ship

Wonderopolis: How Does a Submarine Work?
wonderopolis.org/wonder/How-Does-a-Submarine-Work

INDEX

aircraft carriers, 4, 6, 7, 18

amphibious assault ships, 18, 19

Arleigh Burke destroyers, 14, 15

big decks, 18, 19

hospital ships, 10

hovercrafts, 16

Hunt Class ships, 12

Mercy, 10

mine hunters, 4, 12

submarines, 4, 8, 9

Typhoon, 8, 9

USS *Gerald R. Ford*, 6, 7

Zubr, 16

ABOUT THE AUTHOR

Mari Schuh's love of reading began with cereal boxes at the kitchen table. Today, she is the author of hundreds of nonfiction books for beginning readers. Mari lives in the Midwest with her husband and their sassy house rabbit. Learn more about her at marischuh.com.